The ELEPHANT and the ROPE

A. M. Marcus

4

Will was having trouble with his homework. He tried and tried, but he just couldn't get the right answer. "I can't do this! I'll never be able to!" Will grumbled.

"Maybe I should talk to Grandpa before I just give up. He always knows what to do," Will thought.

8

"What's wrong?" Grandpa asked.
"You look like someone stole
your only piece of candy."

Will laughed, almost forgetting his bad mood. "No, Grandpa. I'm having trouble with my homework. No matter how hard I try, I can't get the right answer. I give up!" he growled.

Grandpa thought for a moment and patted Will's back,

13

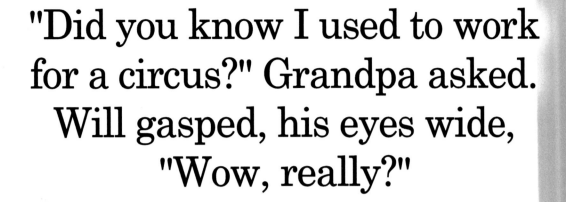

"Did you know I used to work for a circus?" Grandpa asked. Will gasped, his eyes wide, "Wow, really?"

"Yes! Come and sit next to me, and I'll tell you all about it," Grandpa said, motioning to the sofa.

Grandpa began, "I was about 20 years old at the time, and I used to do all sorts of things for the circus. For example, I would make sure the magician's rabbits didn't run away."

"I would help put up the big show tents, and then help take them down afterwards. Sometimes I would even pop the popcorn!" Grandpa said.

Grandpa smiled as he remembered all the great things he used to do, and Will listened carefully, wondering what this had to do with his homework.

"One day, my boss told me to give the elephants a bath. And, let me tell you, it was not an easy job! I had to use a long brush and a lot of soap. Plus I had to watch out for both ends of the elephant!" Grandpa chuckled.

24

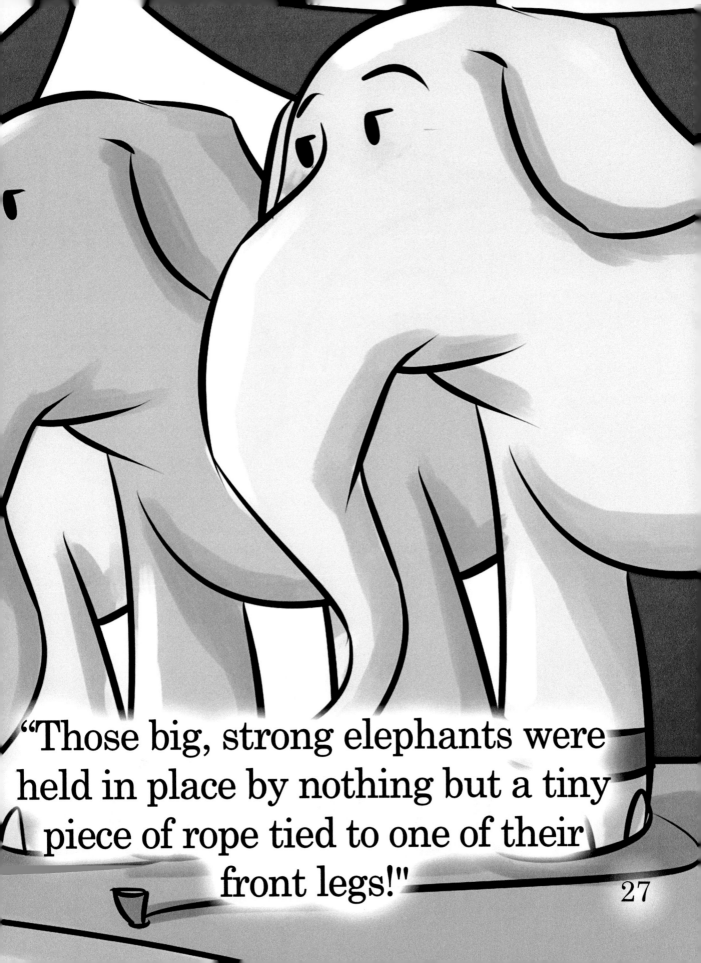

"Those big, strong elephants were held in place by nothing but a tiny piece of rope tied to one of their front legs!"

27

28

"It seemed strange to me, so I found one of the trainers to ask him why the elephants stayed there instead of breaking the rope and running away."

29

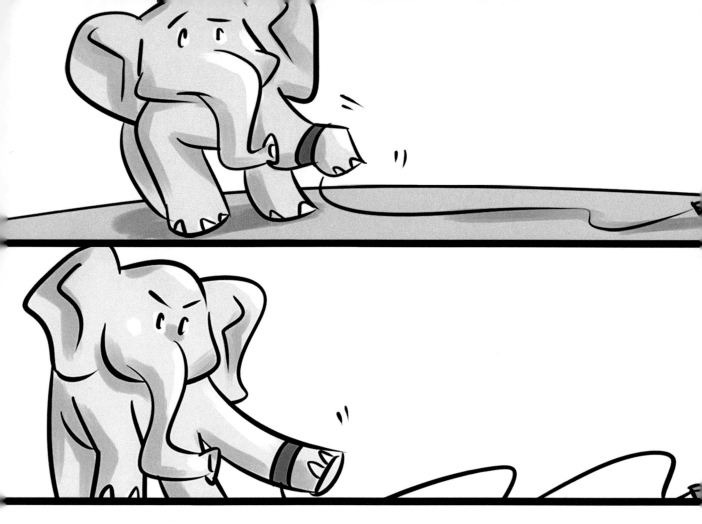

"The trainer told me that when elephants are very young, they tie a small rope around their foot. The young elephants try to break it, but they're still too small and weak. Eventually, they get used to the rope, and as they get bigger, they stop trying!"

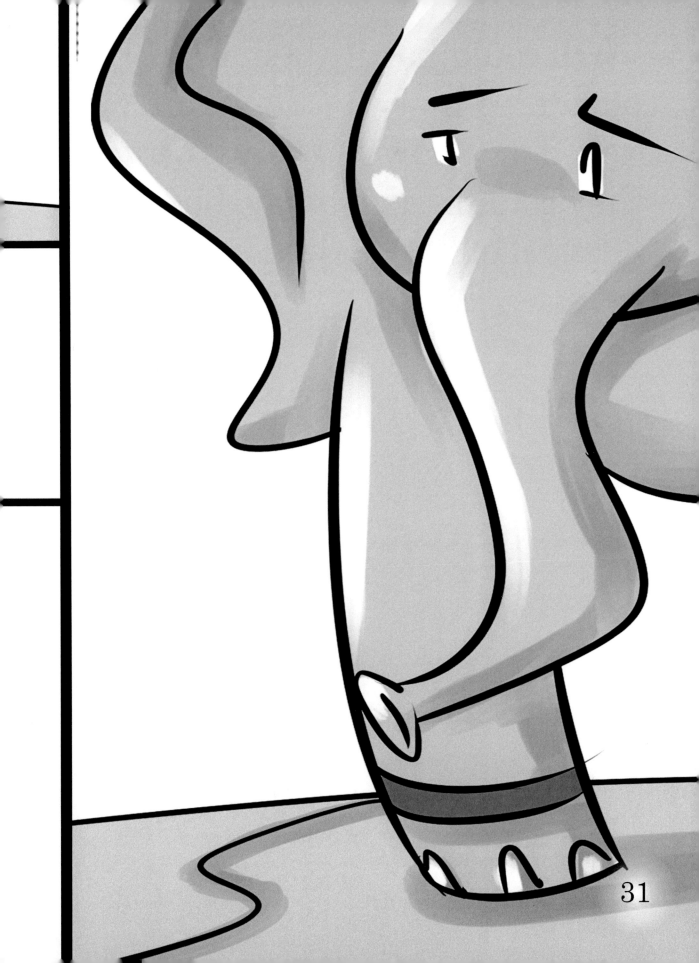

31

Will could hardly believe it! He considered how the elephants were tricked and how they only *thought* they couldn't run away, but could have if only they had just tried!

He realized they had
given up too soon.

33

Grandpa smiled and explained,

34

"You see, just like the elephants, a lot of people go through life hanging on to the belief that they can't do something, simply because they failed at it once before. They forget that you can grow stronger if you just keep pushing yourself to your limits."

Will thought about his homework and how quickly he wanted to quit just because he hadn't been able to do it the first few times.

He decided he wouldn't give up like the elephants and that all he needed to do was keep trying until he could do it.

"Do you understand what I'm trying to teach you?" Grandpa asked.

"Yes! Oh yes, I do!" Will said, and he rushed back to his room, determined to finish his homework. 39

It took him a while, but he kept pushing himself, until at last . . .

He succeeded! He felt like
a big, strong elephant,
breaking the rope that
had held him back.

Will ran back to Grandpa to tell
him the good news!

He gave Will a big hug. "Good job! I'm so proud of you for not giving up. Working hard pays off eventually," Grandpa told him.

The next day at school when Will handed in his homework, he told his class the story about the elephants.

His teacher was very impressed with what he had learned from his Grandpa and she was happy he hadn't given up like the elephants.

At recess, some of the other kids came up to him and asked if he could help them understand their homework.

They wanted to keep trying, just like Will did!

Will smiled as he went to the bench to explain the homework to his classmates.

He was glad he was not like the elephants after all. He was excited to teach his friends what happens if you just persevere.

THE END

Don't forget your FREE GIFT

I remember being your age

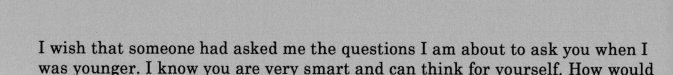

I wish that someone had asked me the questions I am about to ask you when I was younger. I know you are very smart and can think for yourself. How would you answer these questions?

• Do you remember a time when you were trying to do something but it was really hard and you thought you were about to fail? What did you do?

• Is there something you can do very easily now that seemed very hard or even impossible before? How did you get good at this?

• Can you remember something that you completely gave up on because you had failed the first time? Would you like to try again? What would you do differently?

• If you have to face a challenge or something difficult in the future (like starting a new school or playing on a new team), how do you want to act?

I would love to know what you think of my book!
Please send me an email: author@AMMarcus.com
or share your thoughts with the rest of the world on Amazon.

Scan and post a review

A word from me to the grown-ups

Teaching kids the value of hard work and determination is sometimes more important than building self-esteem, and the skill of perseverance is essential to a child's social and emotional development.

Encouraging children to keep working even in the face of mild frustration can give them the important habits needed to accomplish great things in their lives. Modeling, of course, is always important. If our kids see or hear us give up on something because it is too hard, they'll be more likely to share that attitude.

Modeling how you fail, learn from those failures, and are not afraid to try again will encourage your kids to do the same. Don't hide your failures. Even little things like the plumbing disasters and cooking mistakes you've made are learning opportunities. You can show your children that you don't quit but try again. When kids fail, help them turn those feelings into a time to ask questions and try to improve for next time.

If you liked this book would you consider posting a review?
Your help in spreading the word is greatly appreciated. Reviews from readers like you make a huge difference in helping new readers find children's books with powerful lessons similar to this book.

I would love to hear from you! Please subscribe to my email newsletter following the link on the last page. In the newsletter you will find exciting updates, promotions, and more.

Follow this direct link to post a review

go.ammarcus.com/rope-review

Some personal things about me

My favorite fruits: Strawberries & Raspberries

My favorite school subjects: Math & Computers

My favorite hobby: Dancing & Teaching Salsa

My favorite color: Green

My favorite animal: Tiger

My favorite sport: Soccer

My favorite pet: Dogs

Don't forget your
FREE GIFT
on the last page

And a little bit more...

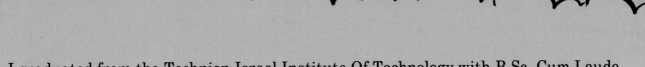

I graduated from the Technion Israel Institute Of Technology with B.Sc. Cum Laude in Computer Engineering. Throughout my studies, I have been teaching and helping children with math, and through my work, I have helped them to discover their inner strength and motivation to continue studying and nurturing success in life.

I love the challenge of early education, and especially enjoy working with children with learning difficulties. I have found great satisfaction in helping them conquer their fears and overcome the challenges associated with their education.

I have read dozens of self-improvement books, and have been influenced heavily by them. Through self-reflection, I have found that my great dream was to share that wisdom and my numerous life lessons with people, but especially with kids.
I left my computer engineering career in order to pursue my dream of becoming an author of children's books. Today, I continue to write these books, with the goal of teaching kids basic skills through storytelling. I believe that a good story is an excellent way to communicate ideas to children.

Each and every story is based upon some deep issue, value, or virtue that can potentially make a huge impact on the lives of both your children and you. I have a vast collection of quotes, and usually I base my stories off quotes that I personally find inspiring. The lesson of this book, for example, can be summed up in the following inspirational quote. Turn the page to check the quote.

www.AMMarcus.com

"A lot of people go through life hanging on to the belief that they can't do something, simply because they failed at it once before."

-Unknown

More books
by A. M. Marcus

    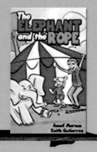

Coming soon!

Don't forget
your FREE GIFT

Scan to get your
FREE GIFT

ammarcus/free-gift

Use the code to get the gift:
584785

Made in the USA
San Bernardino, CA
22 January 2017